A PLACE
like this

steven herrick

Simon Pulse
New York London Toronto Sydney

**Dedicated to Leonie Tyle, Robyn Sheahan,
and Glen Leitch for their support and belief.**

First Simon Pulse edition March 2004

Copyright © 1998 by Steven Herrick
Published by arrangement with University of Queensland Press
Originally published in Australia in 1998 by University of Queensland Press

SIMON PULSE
An imprint of Simon & Schuster
Children's Publishing Division
1230 Avenue of the Americas
New York, NY 10020

Printed in the United States of America

10 9 8 7 6 5 4 3 2 1

Library of Congress Control Number 2003110836

ISBN 0-689-86711-5 (Simon Pule pbk.)

CONTENTS

go

1   Jack   2
2   Jack's Dad   3
3   The stumbling bagpipes   6
4   What Dad said   8
5   For once in my life   10
6   A 1974 Corona   12
7   Annabel on Jack   13
8   Jack driving   15
9   Two days out   16
10 The ride   18

this quiet land

11 Haybales   22
12 The farm   23
13 Craig   24
14 This quiet land   25
15 The shed   26
16 Craig on his Mum   28
17 My Dad says …   30
18 Beck talks   31

screwed

19 Screwed   34

20 School photos   36
21 Colours   37
22 Annabel and babies   38
23 The dew-wet grass   40
24 Lucky Emma   41
25 Emma   43
26 Annabel   44
27 Emma and her Mum   45
28 Lucky   47
29 George   48
30 Like a drunk …   52
31 Emma and the memory   53
32 Staying at school   55
33 Emma's dream   56
34 Sunday Annabel   58
35 Rich, smart, or stupid   60

a place like this

36 Annabel dreams   62
37 Jack   64
38 The Department lady   65
39 Annabel on love   67
40 Emma replies   69
41 He asks   72
42 A gentle kick   74
43 Jack's plans   75
44 Uncle Craig   77
45 Different   78
46 Saturday night   80
47 The snake   82
48 Annabel's snake   84

49   Beck's snake   *85*
50   Naming rights   *86*
51   Cheers   *87*
52   Emma and apples   *88*
53   Emma   *89*
54   Craig hates school   *91*
55   A place like this   *92*

weird

56   Weird   *94*
57   Craig and the cows   *96*
58   Annabel is ready   *97*
59   Jack and the beach   *99*
60   Annabel   *100*
61   Making sense   *101*
62   Annabel and the car   *103*
63   Craig   *104*
64   Birth classes   *105*
65   The perfect sky   *106*
66   Annabel and George   *107*
67   Annabel   *109*
68   Craig and his mad dad   *110*
69   Craig and cricket   *112*
70   Emma and the right way   *113*
71   Guts   *115*
72   Emma and leaving   *117*

a young orchard

73   A young orchard   *120*
74   Annabel   *122*
75   Now   *123*

76 Emma and her Dad   *124*

a full tank

77 Craig knows   *130*
78 It's time   *131*
79 Annabel and the orchard   *133*

warm

80 For the sun   *136*

Go

*J*ack

I'm not unemployed.
I'm just not working at the moment.
School now seems a distant shame
    of ball games, half-lies at lunch time,
    and teachers fearing the worst.
I'm not studying either.
Yeah, I got into Uni,
    so did Annabel.
Two Arts degrees does not a life make.
So we both chucked it.
University is too serious.
I'm eighteen years old,
    too young to work forever
    too old to stay home.
Annabel and I make love most afternoons,
    which, as you can imagine,
    passes the time
    but
I don't think we can make money out of it,
or learn much, although, we have learnt something ...

I want to leave town
I want to leave town
I want to leave.

*J*ack's Dad

What can I tell you about my Dad?
Years ago I would have said
an ill-fitting suit, brown shoes,
a haircut of nightmares,
and a job, in the city.
That's all.
That's what I would have said.
And a dead wife.
Long dead. Dead yesterday.
No difference.

But not now.
Now, he tries.
He reads the paper with courage.
He never shakes his head when I'm late home.
He's forty-two years of hope
        eight years of grief, and
        two years of struggle.

Let me tell you this one thing about my father,
and leave it at that.

Friday night, two months ago.
I'm trying to sleep,
when I hear this soft bounce, every few seconds,
and the backyard floodlight is on.

It's midnight,
and there's a man in the yard.
I grab the cricket bat from the hall cupboard,
check my sister's room, she's asleep,
still in her Levi's and black top
(I like that top — I gave it to her
for her birthday, and she always wears it.
Sorry, I better go bash this burglar ...)

Where's my father when the house needs defending?
At the pub? At work?
Not at midnight surely?
I grip the bat,
wish I'd taken cricket more seriously at school.
I open the door slightly,
think of newspaper headlines —
"HERO DIES SAVING HOUSE"
"CRIME WAVE SOARS OUT WEST"
"HIT FOR SIX!"

There's that bounce again,
and the figure bends to pick something up
(a gun! a knife!)

A cricket ball!
What!

4

He runs and bowls a
slow drifting leg-spinner, hits middle stump.
Dad turns,
whispers "howzat!"
and walks to pick up the ball again.

What can I do?
My Dad, midnight cricket,
and a well-flighted leg-spinner.

I walk out to face up
tapping the bat gently.
Dad smiles and bowls a wrong-un.
The bastard knocks my off-stump out.
He offers me a handshake and advice.
"Bat and pad together son,
   don't leave the gate open.
   Let's have one more over shall we?"

He goes back to his mark,
polishing the ball on his pyjamas,
every nerve twitching,
every breath involved.

The stumbling bagpipes

We make love every Tuesday afternoon.
I kiss her eyelids
and rub my hand along her arm
to feel the soft hair
that shines in the fading light.
Sometimes the clouds float
up the valley
and the rain dances on our window
as the parrots fly for home.
I kiss her shoulders and her neck
and we try breathing slowly, in time,
under the doona.

There's a young boy next door
who's practicing the bagpipes.
He stands on the veranda
and scares hell out of the dogs.
They howl in time
as he blows himself hoarse.

We love that sound,
discordant, clumsy, feverish.
It reminds us of that first Tuesday afternoon,
two years ago,

trying to make love before
Annabel's parents got home.
We agreed on further practice.

That's why we celebrate like this,
every Tuesday,
me and Annabel,
and the stumbling bagpipes.

What Dad said

This is what Dad said
when I told him about me and Annabel
wanting to drive and not come back
for a year or so ...

"Son." (When he says *son* I know a story
    is not far behind.)
"Son. When I was eighteen
I'd already decided to ask your Mum to marry me.
And I had my journalism degree half-finished.
I wanted my own desk, my own typewriter,
a home to put them in, and I wanted your Mum.
She said yes, and the rest followed.
At twenty-two, we had this home.
At twenty-two, I learned gardening.
You know the big golden ash in the corner?
I planted that first year here.
Most of our friends were going overseas,
taking winter holiday work in the snow,
or getting drunk every night at the pub.
At twenty-two, your Mum and I
were sitting on the veranda with a cup of cocoa
and a fruit cake.
I'm fifty-two years old this August.
You're a smart kid Jack. A smart kid.

I think you and Annabel should get out of here
as fast as possible. Have a year doing anything
you want. My going-away present is enough money
to buy a car, a cheap old one OK. You'll have to
work somewhere to buy the petrol, and to keep going.
But go."

Let me tell you
it wasn't what I expected.

But maybe, just maybe,
I understand the old man more now.
More than I ever have.

*F*or once in my life

When Jack told me last night
about leaving
what I really wanted to say
was *NO*.
Like a father should.
NO.
And I had all the words ready,
all the clichés loaded
but I couldn't do it.
He looked so hungry,
so much in need of going
that I gave him my first big speech in years,
only this time it was one he wanted to hear.
So that's it.

When Jack was asleep last night
I went into his room.
I sat beside his bed
      and listened to his breathing.
I don't know for how long.
I listened,
and with each breath
I felt his yearning, and confidence,
and strength.
I walked out of his room
sure I'd said the right thing

maybe not as a father
but as a Dad.
I'd said the right thing,
for once in my life.

A *1974 Corona*

It's a 1974 Corona sedan
that's been driven by a
middle-aged single bank manager
called Wilbur who never went out on the weekend
except for a Sunday morning drive with his Mum
to church five kilometres down the road
and enjoyed cleaning it's dull brown duco
every Saturday instead of
> watching the football
> getting drunk
> doing overtime
> or playing with snappy children.

All I had to do was give him $1200
and a handshake to drive it home,
through a mudpuddle or two,
and take that crucifix off the mirror,
give it to the kid next door,
and maybe even consider a paint job ...

but no, let's leave it brown.
Bank manager brown.
That's my car.
That's my ticket with Annabel, out of here.

Annabel on Jack

Jack reads too many books.
He thinks we're going to drive all year
and have great adventures.
He thinks the little money
we have will last.
He wants to sleep in the car,
cook dinner over an open fire.
I'm just waiting for him to
pack a fishing line, smiling,
saying "we can live off the land".
Jesus Christ.
I'm not gutting a fish and cooking it.
But
I do want to go,
even if it only lasts a month or two.
Even if we drive to Melbourne and back
and don't talk to another person.
I want to go.
Why?
Because I've never
been more than 200 kilometres from home,
and that was with my parents, on holiday.
And because Jack's smart,
but not that smart, if you know what I mean.
You watch.
First week, we'll be out of money,

sleeping near a smelly river,
eating cold baked beans out of a can.
The car will have a flat battery
and Jack will be saying something like,
"Isn't this great. Back to nature.
Living off the land. Not a care in the world."
Jesus Christ.

*J*ack driving

I love to drive,
to blast back to boyhood
where I dreamt of a highway,
a car with a floor-shift
and nowhere to sleep for a week,
burning rubber and a dare
to take every bend
faster than advised.
Even now
I think of a blow-out
as a test for how steady
my hands are on the wheel,
my knuckles white with impatience.
Me, Annabel and
the stereo sing,
trucks threaten our dreams
like thunder,
as we reach the hill
curse the oncoming lights,
I strain to keep the revs up
as we crest the rise,
I snap into top
glide down the mountain
escape ramp 500 metres ahead,
we don't need it.

*T*wo days out

Two days out.
Last night we slept in the car.
Yes, by a river, as I predicted.
Not smelly though.
Clean. Surprisingly clean.
Jack and I had a bath in it.
A naked goose pimple bath.
We raced each other from bank to bank.
We even used soap.
My Mum's going-away present.
Soap-on-a-rope. It floats!

We lay on the grass.
The sun dried our white bodies.
We did nothing for as long as possible.

In the quiet afternoon
we drove for hours.
Jack said, "I'm hungry"
and the bloody car slowed to a stop.
Jack looking at me,
me at Jack,
and neither of us knowing why.
Then I looked at the petrol gauge.
Empty.

Empty, and food, cold river baths
and the nearest town
were all a million miles away.
Two days out ...

As I stood on the lonely backroad,
I'm sure I heard birds,
kookaburras,
laughing ...

*T*he ride

"You two heading anywhere special?"
he says, changing down gear, double-clutching
and churning the old truck's insides loud.
Annabel and I look at each other.
What's this mean?
I decide to answer a question with a question.
I learnt that in Year 9
and it hasn't failed me yet.
"Why?"

"Why. Because I got fifty acres of ripe apples
and a town full of unemployed kids that
hate the sight of them, that's why.
And my kids and I can't pick fifty acres
in two years, much less two months.
I'll pay you, give you a place to sleep.
That's if you're interested?"

The truck cabin rattles over potholes.
He winds down the window
and flicks his cigarette out.

It's not what I'm expecting.
Two days away, out of petrol, and offered a job.
I wanted to get as far as possible,
not a few hundred kilometres down the road.

But it's money. And a place to stay.
Annabel squeezes my hand and I know
it's a *yes* squeeze.
I squeeze back and before I can answer
Annabel says,
'Sure mister. We'll take it. I like apples."

George smiles and says,
"You'll be picking Miss, not eating them."

But he's all right.
Anyone who drives a truck this old can't be too bad.

This Quiet Land

*H*aybales

It was from a book I read in school.
Two teenagers and a shed full
     of stacked haybales,
a crow's nest in the loft,
and her father, the farmer, in town.
I can't remember anything else but
these two, barely fifteen years old,
lying up high on the bales
and the boy with his hand
     up her dress,
and they're both shaking,
even though it's summer outside.
She takes off her dress,
her bra, and undies,
stands on the highest bale
and gestures him up.
And in a tumble of straw and clothes
they made nervous love
page after page.
First from his side,
     all awkward, lopsided, and flush.
Then hers,
     sweat and itch and eyes on the crow's nest.
I kept that book for years.
And when George offered us his shed to sleep in,
I said *yes*,
and asked if it had haybales …

The farm

The road goes through a path of pines.
It's dusty and hot, but here, for a while,
the trees hold the cool and dark,
then a sharp left and you see the wooden house,
surrounded by wattles and a sagging fence.
Two kids run out,
no more than ten years old,
both jump on the tray while the truck's still moving,
country kids.
There's someone else, older,
sixteen maybe, a girl,
standing in the dirt of the drive,
wearing overalls and dusty riding boots,
and when we turn to park near the shed,
I see she's pregnant.
George says, "that's Emma, my eldest",
as the four dogs start barking all at once,
sniffing our hands and boots,
and running around George, jumping up,
and not stopping barking,
not for a second.

Craig

I'm Craig. I'm ten next week.
You come to pick apples for us?
You gunna stay? Lots don't stay,
reckon it's too hard.
Reckon Dad don't pay enough.
Reckon we're stupid to live this far from town.
You gunna stay?
We need help, Dad says.
Now Emma can't pick.
She's pregnant you know.
Gunna have twins, or three, or four.
She's so big. Bigger than a cow.
Bigger than a house.
She couldn't climb the ladder to pick now.
You ever picked before?
I can pick two bins a day.
I reckon it's good for football training.
You two married?
You're not gunna get pregnant are you?
Anyway, I'll see ya.
My sister's name is Beck, she's seven.
She don't talk much.
Not like me.
See ya.

*T*his quiet land

It's nothing more than an irrigation channel
dug across the plains,
but George, despite his eye on the harvest
    and it's price,
years before built a hardwood landing
to dive off into the cool water.
Annabel and I spend every afternoon
    after picking
lying on the wet timber
    listening to the frogs
and watching the dragonflies skim across the surface.

What can I say?
When we know George is in town
    or too busy hosing down the tractor
we strip naked and worship the late breeze
blowing ripples across the channel.
A beer or two and I'm set for life.
A beer or two and Annabel's lips
    and her arm resting on my stomach
    and I hope to never leave
the late afternoon
    of tired muscles, channel water,
    and this quiet land.

*T*he shed

Me and Annabel are sitting against the shed.
In the sun.
Sunday. No work.
I'm dreaming of a month of Sundays.
We've been working for two weeks.
Our hands are starting to heal
    from the first week of learning
    to snap the stem of each apple
    as we plucked it.
    Yes, "pluck", that's what George says.
George loves his apples so much
    he can't bear to just pick them.
    He plucks them quick, yet soft,
    places them in his bag
    and when it's full
    leans over the bin and releases the latch.
He fills four, sometimes five bins a day.
That first week Annabel and I averaged three together,
from 7am to 5pm. Climbing ladders with the bag
half-full,
swinging in front, pulling your neck forward.
I cursed my luck for running out of petrol.

The second week was easier.
George gave us the heavy trees, loaded down,
until the weight broke the branches.

We filled four bins a day. By Friday, it was five.
Twenty Dollars a bin.
George says we're all right.
So "alright" last night he came into the shed
with a dozen bottles of beer.

I like the sun when I'm tired.
I lay down,
close my eyes and think of
anything but apples.

Craig on his Mum

Mum ran away from us
the night Beck vomited all over the dinner.
She didn't take much,
except the blind cat and all our money.
Well, that's what Dad said.
Beck vomited all over everyone's dinner.
It was unreal. I don't know if that's why Mum left,
but she left,
and for weeks I kept thinking she was hiding
somewhere on the farm,
in the shed,
or camping down by the channel,
and I kept hoping she'd just
come walking back into the kitchen,
but that hasn't happened.

I'm learning to cook now.
So is Beck.
We get our own breakfast and lunch,
and sometimes we cook dinner —
you know, spaghetti and some sauce,
from a jar.
Emma can cook, pretty good too.
I miss Mum sometimes,
and I know Beck does too,
but Beck hasn't vomited since.

Not at the dinner table or anywhere,
and Mum might come back one day.
Dad says she won't.
He doesn't say much about her,
which is funny because they
must have been pretty friendly,
don't you reckon,
to get married and all.

I'm not getting married.
I'm not having kids who vomit all over the dinner.
But I might run away from here,
when I'm older.
I might even go look for Mum.

My Dad says ...

My Dad says you're good workers.
He says you're the best he's had in years.
He says he doesn't care what you do in our shed,
as long as you keep working the same.
He said that last night at dinner.
I asked him what you do in our shed,
and Emma laughed.
She hasn't laughed in a while
and then she says,
"Yeah Dad, tell Craig what they're doing."
But Dad doesn't.
He tells Beck not to eat so fast,
probably scared of her vomiting again.
He tells me to mind my own business,
but Dad tells me that at least once a day,
so it's nothing new.
And that's why I'm here now.
So you tell me, OK,
what do you do in our shed here?

*B*eck talks

My brother Craig,
he thinks he knows everything,
but
he doesn't know who let the dog
wee in his football boots ...

I know.

Screwed

Screwed

I got screwed.
That's how I got pregnant.
Screwed.
If you want to know, I'll tell you.
The truth.
Not what I told Dad.
"My boyfriend, Dad."
The one I made up.
The one who had to leave town with his parents
on account of his father's work.
What a load of bull.
What boyfriend.
We live twenty kilometres from town.
The school bus is our only link.
School buses don't take you anywhere after 3pm.
So one Friday I arranged to stay
at my friend Jenny's place.
The Friday her parents are away,
and we have a party.
All of Year 10.
A big party. A loud party.
And I drink too much,
even dance a bit, just to show myself I can.
I'm drinking away
the twenty kilometres of loneliness out here.
I'm drinking away

the exam results that don't take me anywhere.
I'm drinking away
my clothes that smell of this farm.
I'm drinking away
apples, apple pie, baked apples, apple juice,
apple jam for God's sake.
Then I pass out,
feeling pretty good really.

I passed out on Jenny's lounge.
In the morning I woke on her parent's bed,
with no clothes on.

I got screwed.
I got pregnant.
And I didn't even get to enjoy
becoming this big and ugly.
And nobody in Year 10 knows a thing.
Nobody, that is,
except one person.

School photos

I've been going through my school photos.
Every one since Year 5.
I'm making a list of each boy's features.
Big nose, blond hair, freckles, ears that stick out.
I've got twenty-one boys from Year 10
going back for years.
What a bunch of uglies,
and watching them get uglier every year
are all my girlfriends.
The girls who didn't see anything at Jenny's party.
None of them wear glasses,
so maybe they were just blind drunk.
Blind drunk. Or too scared to remember anything.
Twenty-one boys. Twenty-one prospective fathers.
Ten with blond hair.
Ten with dark hair.
And nerdy Phillip Montain with
red hair, freckles, and ... surely not!

It may take years of comparing their features
with that of my baby,
but when I do,
and I know,
well,
someone's going to get screwed,
and, this time,
it won't be me.

Colours

It's the sky I love.
Annabel and I sunbathe
on the hardwood landing of the channel.
I spend hours lost
in the deep summer blue
that goes forever.
I remember being a kid,
me and Dad climbing
onto our roof and looking up.
I'd dream we were flying
and all summer
I'd never want to land.
Annabel and I imagine
animals in the clouds, like kids do,
as a distant jet
writes across the sky
longer than history
and I lay back
remember being a kid again
lost in the innocent colours
of childhood.

Annabel and babies

I think about babies.
My baby, when and if.
Emma's baby, twenty kilometres from town,
no Dad, but lots of apple mush for food.
Jack and me with a baby.
I'm not serious,
I'm just thinking,
passing this Saturday while Jack works
on our car that goes nowhere, but goes nowhere well.
When I left school and got into Uni
I thought my life was made.
Uni, job, money, Jack, travel, house,
Jack, more travel,
and still Jack.
Jack was the constant.

Then one weekend he says
he's quitting.
He wants to drive, anywhere,
as long as it's away from Uni and home.
He wants me to come.
That night my room seemed so small
like a kids room, full of toys and stuff
and none of it meant anything.
I picked up my textbooks
and tried reading them,

and I realised for five years
I'd been reading books that didn't make sense,
and now, I had four more years of it.

I went downstairs and told Mum and Dad.
It's one Sunday they won't forget.
Dad raved, Mum cried.
Then Dad asked *why*?
And all I could answer was
    because I'm too young to decorate a home
    because text books have really bad covers
    because I don't want to wear neat clothes
      and wake every morning at 7.30
    because Jack and I have never been wrong yet
and because I want a year for myself, not my future.

So, late Sunday, we did a deal.
My Dad, the solicitor, bargained
a year off, a deferment,
then back to the books.
I agreed. What else could I do?
And now,
I'm thinking about babies.
Emma's baby.
Jack and my baby.
Growing in my mind, if not in my womb.

The dew-wet grass

The best time is early morning
with the dew-wet grass,
the hills shouldered in mist,
everything quiet.
Annabel and I climb each ladder,
pick a cold apple
and crunch away.
The juice so sharp and tart
it hurts my teeth.
We sit like this,
watching the crows in the fir trees,
the silver-eyes darting among the fruit,
listening for George's tractor
with the empty bins rattling,
calling to be filled.
Annabel, the mist, a farm apple, the birds,
and an orchard waking up.

Lucky Emma

Sometimes
I feel like someone
who's won the smallest prize in the lottery
but lost the ticket.
I think of all the Year 10 boys.
Mark Spencer with his long hair,
black silverchair T-shirt,
leaning back in his chair
playing air-guitar all through Maths.
Peter Borovski and his love affair with himself.
     "Hey Peter, who you sleeping with tonight?
     You're kidding. Yourself again.
     What I'd give for your luck.
     And confidence. And stupidity."
Luke Banfield, who once this year talked to a girl,
yeah, once. He asked her if she'd seen his basketball.
I was that lucky girl.
Or maybe, just maybe,
Steve Dimitri, one of the few fifteen year olds I know
who can eat with his mouth closed
who doesn't know how to play basketball
who doesn't look at the ground when talking to a girl
and who doesn't vomit after three drinks.
He vomits after five drinks ...

Actually, I take back what I said.
I feel like someone
who's won the smallest prize in the lottery,
found the ticket
and has to collect the winnings
even though
she doesn't want them.

Emma

I wish I had a boyfriend like you.
Someone who wanted to be with me,
all the time.
It's true.
I watch you two in the orchard.
Every ten minutes he stops picking
to look where you are.
Sometimes you see him, sometimes not,
but he's there, checking you out.
He's not my physical type mind,
but,
I'd love to have someone like that.
And someone to sleep with.
What's that like?
Every night. Does he hold you?
Does he snore?
Does he kiss you before sleep?
God! I've been watching too many soap operas,
but I'd like to know.
The only person I've slept with
is bloody Craig when he was scared one night.
He spent all night dropping silent bombers
under the blankets. What a brother!
Yeah, I'd like a boyfriend,
but I don't like my chances at the moment.
You're a lucky girl,
you know that.

*A*nnabel

It hurt,
listening to Emma talk like that.
It's like some bad dream,
pregnant,
and she didn't even have sex,
well, not really.
It's not the Immaculate Conception though.

I like her.
She's upfront.
She's taking it better than I would.
I'd buy a gun and shoot all twenty-one boys, on suspicion.
And then Jack and I come along,
making love every night in her shed,
and she notices stuff, about Jack.
I've stopped noticing.
She makes me grateful.
I'm going to drive into town later
and buy Jack something,
a CD, or a new shirt maybe.
I might buy Emma
a dress, normal-size,
for after the baby.
A new dress to show the world
on her one trip to town every month.
Her one trip to town, for groceries.

*E*mma and her Mum

Mum and I were cooking
the Sunday before she left.
She stopped blending, and sifting,
she looked out the window
at the day
and I remember it was hot
with not a breath of wind.
Craig and Beck were outside
fighting over whose turn it was
to ride the bike.
Mum looked out, past them,
past the sagging fence,
and the tree-line,
and she said,
"A farm takes a lot out of you,
  sometimes too much."
I thought she was just complaining,
or dreaming,
so I didn't question her.
And that night
Beck vomited all over the Sunday dinner.
That was our last meal together.

When I think of Mum and what she did
I get stiff in this chair
and I look out the same window,

past the same fence, over the same tree-line,
and I touch my stomach
and I whisper,
"I won't ever leave you
  I won't ever ..."

*L*ucky

George thinks we're mad.
Emma thinks we're mad.
Craig and Beck think it's cool
sleeping on a bed of haybales
five metres from the ground
a thin foam mattress
to cover the hay
and blankets, lots of them
piled up high.
Annabel and I climb
the haybale stairs
and feel like King and Queen.
Sometimes we hear the possums
scurrying across the roof
and the birds nesting
in the rusted gutters
and late at night
when the farm sleeps
I hear Annabel's breathing,
a distant owl, and the
slow rhythm of the
windvane on the farmhouse roof.
George and Emma are wrong.
We're not mad, we're lucky.

George

George talks about the weather,
he talks about apples,
sometimes, when he's in a good mood,
he talks about his kids.
This is one of those times.
Lunch in the orchard.
Packed sandwiches and a thermos of tea.
Annabel and I sit against the tractor.
George squats in the shade of a tree
and talks,
"Good kids, all of them.
Sure Craig never shuts up,
but what ten-year-old does?
And he's strong.
He helps out around the place.
He'll try and lift anything.
Poor kid will have a hernia before he's a teenager!
And Beck's sweet. She always calls me Dadda.
And I feel like a real Dad when I read to her at night.
She won't sleep without one story, at least.
She's quiet, like me, but smarter.
And Emma, angry with the world.
You can see it, can't you?
But then, she's got reason to be."

George's voice trails off.
We both keep quiet.
He'll tell us if he wants.
"When she first told me,
I wanted to get my gun.
Yeah, I know,
just what you'd expect from a father.
And I would have,
if her mother was around.
I would have made a big show of being angry,
shouted, stormed around looking for bullets,
vowing to chase the kid out of town.
But without Emma's mother here
it seemed pointless.
So I sat and talked, and listened too.
I'm glad I did.
She dismissed the boy, whoever it was.
Someone who's left town.
Some boyfriend I never knew.
You know, I'm still not sure
if she's telling me the truth,
or if she's protecting somebody,
but, it doesn't matter.
What matters is the kid.
I keep telling myself that.
I don't think of becoming a grandad.

I just think of my little girl
becoming a Mum.
Sometimes I wish her mother was here,
for the baby. For Emma.
Not for me.
Emma's mother is dead for me.
She died the day she left."

George looks at us,
as if he's just noticed we're here.
I'm sure he'd been working all that stuff
through these last few months,
here in the orchard,
and it's finally out.

"I talk too much.
She's not dead.
But I'm glad of one thing.
When she left, I'm glad she took her clothes,
her jewellery, even most of the money,
and, by Christ,
I'm glad she left me the kids.
I'd be lost without them.
Lost and bitter.
With them here, I'm only bitter."

George gets up,
tips the tea out under a tree,
packs the esky with what's left
and says,
"Come on, the apples won't pick themselves.
You two are good workers.
I hope you'll stay for the season.
You'll see Emma's baby too, maybe.
By the way, have you ever seen a baby being born?"

Now that was something for Annabel and me
to think of all afternoon.

*L*ike a drunk ...

The night of the day
George told us about seeing the baby
Annabel and I got drunk.
We sat on our favourite haybales
and drank beer, cold and bitter
straight from the bottle.
As the evening light dimmed
we climbed into our makeshift bed
and made noisy love,
like farm animals in the barn
like a drunk falling into a pub, penniless
like a bird caught in the crosshair of a gun
like a truck with no brakes, half-way down a hill
like a kid with a match and a paddock of dry grass
like George without a wife
like Emma without a lover
like a baby, crying to be born.

*E*mma and the memory

Sometimes,
I think I can feel it happening.
I mean,
I can remember how it felt.
It wasn't the pain,
not real pain, like when you cut your hand,
or tread on a rusty nail, or anything,
more an irritation,
a dull irritation,
pressing on me.
And I can smell it too,
like dirty socks left in the laundry basket too long,
and stale beer, but that was probably me.
And I can taste salt, my own tears?
I wasn't crying surely? I was passed out!
Maybe he was crying, the bastard.
I hope he was. Crying with shame.
The only woman he could get was unconscious.
The thought gives me pleasure, at least.
That's all.
I lie in bed, thinking of how it felt.
Not knowing if it's my imagination,
or suppressed memory,
or what really happened.

I remember waking up.
I walked into Jenny's bathroom and vomited.
Only then did I realise I was naked.
Naked, sore, wet, sticky,
and slowly becoming
very, very
suspicious.

Staying at school

Dad says I should have stayed at school,
should have kept going right up to the day.
Now wouldn't that be a sight,
me in a school uniform.
Size 18 wouldn't even fit this belly.
And Personal Development classes
would have had special meaning, don't you think.
Me, six months pregnant,
learning about the correct use of condoms
and other devices,
and you know what I would have said
to that Mrs Barber, our teacher,
as she was showing us condoms on carrots?
I would have put my hand up right there,
and said,
"Miss, how do you keep from getting pregnant
   when you're passed out drunk
     and someone takes advantage?"
It would almost be worth going back to school
just to ask that one question ...

*E*mma's dream

Sometimes, when I'm asleep,
I have a dream where
I'm living in a city,
going to work in fancy clothes,
and I have a boyfriend,
and a house of my own
on a normal city street,
you know,
with neighbours, and a shop down the road,
and the only animal is a pet dog,
and the only trees are for shade,
or flowers, or decoration.
In this dream
I go out to the movies
with my boyfriend
and we eat dinner
in a restaurant,
and on weekends I don't have to do anything
but enjoy myself.
And in this dream
I'm walking to work on Monday
and I'm nearly there,
and I remember the baby,
my baby,
and it gets kind of strange
in my dream

because I'm standing outside my work
trying to remember
if I have a baby
or not,
and where it is,
and that's when
I'm not sure
if my dream
is a dream,
or a nightmare.

Sunday Annabel

Another Sunday of sunshine,
no work, and swimming in the channel.
Emma sits by the bank
watching Jack swing from the rope
and drop into a welcome of still water.
I'm lying here, soaking up a day off,
listening to the sound of nothing
but Jack being a kid again.
Emma talks about school,
and her days on this farm
and how she wants to leave
and every time she mentions leaving
I notice her hands touching her stomach.
I listen and silently vow
to not mention Jack and I leaving
as soon as the work's done.
I tell Emma about where we live
in the suburbs
and the sounds we hear
and the neighbours,
and how Jack and I
just had to get out,
to end up here.
Emma looks up quick when I say this,
and I know what she's thinking.
She knows we can leave when we want.

At that moment Jack falls between us
and starts shaking the water off himself,
like a mad dog,
looking for some attention.

Rich, smart, or stupid

You must be rich, smart,
or real stupid you two.
That's what Emma says.
She says only way you could be doing this
is to be rich, smart, or stupid.
She says most people would have to stay home,
study, or work, or have babies maybe.
She says you two get to drive around the place,
work when you want —
she thinks that makes you smart.
And you don't worry about money.
You buy beer whenever,
you buy each other presents,
you go into town and eat —
she thinks that makes you rich.
She says you're rich and smart
but
she says
you're staying here by choice
when you could drive away.
You're staying here working in the orchard,
and sleeping in a shed.
She says that makes you stupid.

A Place Like This

*A*nnabel dreams

It comes in the late afternoon.
I'm in the orchard,
halfway up the ladder,
my neck aching with the weight of the bag
stretching to reach one full red apple,
and I suddenly think of University.
 The afternoon lecture,
 fifty of us, all dressed in jeans & T-shirts
 taking notes
 searching for the phrase that will guarantee
 good exam results.
 Pages and pages,
 and I'd stop for a second
 to touch my forehead.
 I'd feel the small furrow
 between my eyes,
 deepening, it seems,
 with every afternoon lecture.
I sit on the ladder,
rest the bag on the lower rung
hold that apple, rub it along my cheek,
my forehead, smoothing away my past,
and I take long slow crunching bites
as the afternoon breeze

wakens the silver-eyes in the branches,
and I spend all my education
on doing nothing but eating and watching
for just long enough
to feel clean again.

*J*ack

We came here for the money.
George happened along at the right time.
We had no petrol, nowhere to stay,
and no plans.
When I think about it we had to say yes.
It was that, or go home,
with nothing.
I keep feeling I owe George,
and his children.
I know about the quiet revolution
in every family.
I think of my sister and me eight years ago,
waiting, knowing our Mum was going to die.
Knowing, even at our age.
It took me years to work out what to think,
where to put that stuff.
And I look at Emma here,
and George, the strain in his eyes,
and his voice.
I know where it's coming from
and it won't go away, not for awhile.
I'm glad we came here.
I work extra hard in the orchard,
not for the money anymore,
but for something I can't explain.
Something worth more than money.

The Department lady

I got a visitor from town yesterday,
the Department lady.
Talking about after the baby's born.
What I can get to help.
Money? Not enough.
Health Care. "Don't worry, he won't get sick," I said.
And New Mothers' Monday meeting
where everyone talks about
how beautiful their baby is.
I put a stop to that one.
I asked her if the Department would give me a car,
you know,
to make the meeting on time.
Then she asked me about school.
If I wanted to go back.
I could get money.
I could get my Leaving Certificate.

I wanted to ask her about it,
but she was such a cow.

She started packing up.
Her visit over. The government's job done.
And I didn't like her.
The way she looked at the old lino in the kitchen,
and the dirty dishes,

and she never looked me in the eye,
she looked at her paperwork,
then at our cheap living,
and she asked too many questions.

So when she said goodbye,
I said there was one thing she could do,
I looked at her straight,
the way I'm looking at you now,
and I said,
"You could find out who the father is,
    that'd be a big help ..."

She didn't have an answer for that.
People like her only ever have questions.

Annabel on love

Mine was Year 10.
Jack.
After the movies, at my doorstep,
like a stupid Romance novel.
He kissed me. Nice, but quick.
From my bedroom window
I saw him walking home
and I wanted more.
More was months later.

What can I say?
It's embarrassing now to remember.
He felt heavy and awkward,
lying on top of me.
I'm trying to kiss him,
but his mind's elsewhere.
He's trying to put it in,
and he can't,
so I reached down
and did it for him, simple.

And do you know what was the best bit?
Afterwards.
When he lay in me, limp,
and we held each other,
and started kissing again,

slow and soft, no pressure,
and we started giggling
and kissing still
and touching each other,
relieved it was over,
so now we could start
to really make love,

and we haven't stopped.

*E*mma replies

In Year 9 I kissed a boy,
after school.
Netball training cancelled,
and me alone, shooting hoops,
with an hour to spare, waiting for Dad.
And Rick Harvey comes over,
starts shooting with me.
Offers me a game of keyring,
twenty cents a basket,
and he wins a few,
I win a few.
He owes me forty cents,
when I know he's got no money
or no desire to give me money,
but he's all right
and we sit against the clubhouse
close enough,
and he leans over and starts kissing me.
No questions, no waiting,
and it's OK
so I kiss back.
For a while we just sit there,
our lips pressing,
then I feel his hand
on my leg
tracing a path up

and he's soft and gentle really
so I let him touch me,
you know, there,
outside my pants,
then inside,
and he's not pushy or anything,
and we're both very quiet now,
we've stopped kissing really,
our lips are just together,
our minds are down below, up my dress,
and he puts his finger inside me
and I like it,
and he keeps touching me
inside and out
and soon all I'm thinking of is my body.
I'm hardly sure he's there,
it's me and my body
and I don't move a muscle
in case it all stops
and he keeps doing the same thing
for minutes, for hours
for God knows.
I loved it.
I tell you
it was Christmas, and Easter,
and chocolate cake, and dreams,

and birthdays
and it wasn't Rick Harvey

it was me.
Me and my body,
waking up.

*H*e asks

A funny thing happened today.
In town.
I was in Penney's Department store,
looking at baby clothes,
but daydreaming really.
Thinking how am I going to learn
to be a good mum.
You know, stuff like what to feed him,
or her,
what to do if they look sick,
or hot, or cold, or they cry too much.
I'm thinking all this
as I look through the baby clothes I can't afford
when someone behind me says hello.
It's Adam Barlow, from school. Year 10.
He's in his uniform,
shirt hanging out as usual
socks down, bunched over his sneakers.
He looks nervous,
here in the baby section of Penney's.
He asks how I've been.
He asks how long before the baby's born.
He asks what it's like on the farm
          with no school to worry.
He asks if I know what I'll call it.
He asks what my Dad thinks.

He asks if I'll come back to school afterwards.
He asks again how I've been.
Then he says he's got to go.
He asks far too many questions,
and he answers none.

A *gentle kick*

As Adam Barlow
walked out of Penney's yesterday
I felt my baby kick.
A gentle tap really,
as if my child
was reminding me
of what's important
and what's not
as Adam Barlow
walked out.

*J*ack's plans

This is not what I planned.
I wanted lonely beaches with Annabel
and bush camping
beside a river
and maybe even time in the snow
working for a season
amongst the wealthy.
Not here,
jump-starting tractors
sleeping in a shed
working ten-hour days
and now, get this,
going to birth classes
with Emma and Annabel!
I'm eighteen years old
and going to birth classes
for a girl who's not my girlfriend
for a baby that's not mine
and I've got to admit
yes
when I think about it
I've got to admit
I'm looking forward to it!

Emma deserves help,
like George needed help with picking.

And one day,
maybe one day,
Annabel and I will want a baby.
God!
I'm starting to sound like my Dad.
Birth classes.
God!
I hope I don't have to touch anything.
Or lay on my back and breathe funny ...

Uncle Craig

I hope Emma has the baby at home.
I want to see it,
you know,
being born.
I've seen calves, and lambs,
and even a piglet being born,
but never a real baby.
I reckon it'll be unreal.
Emma says after I was born
I cried for days.
She said I'd never shut up
which is funny really
because Dad says I never shut up now
so maybe that's what happens,
you get born and act the same
your whole life.
Anyway, I'm being real nice to Emma now,
so she'll let me watch
and you know
it means I'll be an uncle,
at my age.
It'll be unreal.

Different

You two are different.
Different than my school friends.
They want to know about the baby, sure,
but only because they're not pregnant
and only because they've got nothing else to say,
not since Jenny's party anyway.
They don't want to know about me.
And how it feels
     to be carrying this great weight
     to be a mother without a boyfriend
     to be missing school, and parties,
     and all of my friends.

I'm glad you're here.
I'm glad you're coming with me to my classes.
I couldn't go alone,
and I need to know stuff
     about the birth.
Truth is, I'm scared.
I'm sure Dad's truck won't start.
Or the ambulance won't come.
Or the midwife.
Or I'll be home alone
with everyone in the orchard.
And the pain,
and how long it'll take.

It's kind of funny really.
Jenny, Peter, Rick Harvey,
even Adam bloody Barlow
are hard at it studying
for their exams
and I'm here
about to study
for something much bigger ...
I hope I pass.

Saturday night

The drunk night.
George in town.
The farmhouse asleep.
Annabel and me on the haybales,
stacked high.
We can almost touch the roof.
A bottle of wine,
a dozen beers,
and all night.
Drinking and telling stories,
like
your first embarrassing moment,
the day you learnt Santa wasn't real,
the first time you vomited,
the day you learnt your parents
    did more than just sleep together,
and the first time you got drunk.

Hours of stories,
here, above the farm
on our haybales.

At midnight
Annabel took off all her clothes
    without saying a word,

then asked for another glass of beer, please.
So beautiful, and so well-mannered.

What could I do?
I took a long drink
and undressed.
Annabel cheered
as we stood,
straining to touch the roof,
from our naked haybale world.

The snake

It was two metres long,
brown and mean,
and coming after the chickens.
I nearly stepped on the thing,
and, yes, it was probably as scared as me,
but I jumped higher,
and I picked up the shovel leaning against the shed
and hit it hard,
once, right in the middle,
and again on it's head,
and again and again,
until I was sure,
and again because I'd never be sure,
and then I felt sick
and I ran behind the shed to vomit.
Nothing but green bile came up,
green bile and tears.

I walked back
and George was inspecting it.
A King Brown.
Annabel came out and saw it too.
And Craig. And Beck.
The farm dogs still barked at it,

too late now to be of any use.
Everyone standing out in the sun
looking at the snake,
except Annabel,
who's looking at me.

Annabel's snake

All night, in the shed,
I held Jack.
He was sweating in the chill air,
waking every hour, jerking his legs,
as if running.
I held his arms, tight.
I could feel the muscles tense,
wanting to move,
wanting to flex,
so I held him.
I didn't sleep much, maybe an hour.
Most of the night,
I watched Jack
strike that snake
a thousand times over
and not once, in his sleep,
did that snake die.

*B*eck's snake

After it was all over
I picked it up
took it down to the garden
and I buried it
deep in the ground
where it's quiet
where it's safe
where the dogs can't get it.

Naming rights

I'm going to call him Joseph,
or Josephine if it's a girl.
Why?
Because it's a strong name,
Joe, Joseph.
You give a kid a name like Cameron
or Alfred, or something like that,
and they end up wearing glasses
and looking at computers for the rest of their life.
And Matthew and Nathan
enter school with another
fifteen Matthews and Nathans beside them.
So Joe it is.
He'll turn out strong. Strong and smart.
And I thought of Joseph, you know,
in the Bible.
Him and Mary and Immaculate Conception.
Well, I reckon my baby's conception
was pretty damn immaculate.
And I couldn't call the kid Jesus,
could I?
Joseph.
Josephine.

Cheers

It's six weeks since we left home.
Our great adventure ran out of petrol
and stopped on this farm.
The harvest is nearly done.
George looks happier,
he lets me drive the tractor,
he lets us finish early on Friday.
He even let Emma come to town with us last Saturday.
We watched the local football.
Big farmers tackling even bigger truckies
and their sons, stepping effortlessly
around them all.
A few of Emma's friends came up to say hello.
They all asked the same questions.
Baby this, baby that.
Emma only existed as the baby-carrier it seems.
They all looked slightly guilty,
especially the girls,
as though a bond had been broken,
or something, I don't know.
We sat on the bonnet of our car
and clapped
when someone scored a try,
and we all cheered whenever
Adam Barlow got tackled.
Emma, Annabel, and I
cheered the game,
and cheered ourselves.

*E*mma and apples

I needed to get away from the farm,
if only for a day.
People say apples have no smell,
well, even now,
twenty kilometres away,
I can still smell them.
I'll smell them when I'm dead, I reckon.
If you stay too long on the farm
you'll get the same, for sure.
It's alright for Craig.
He wants to be a farmer,
he's got apple juice for blood.
And Beck? She'll escape
on her brains, I bet.
But me? Where do I fit?
Not on the farm,
not in a one-pub town
like this,
not anywhere I guess.
Maybe in a city,
where I can get lost,
get lost for good.

Emma

After the football on Saturday,
when Jack, Annabel and me
got back into the car,
I had this urge to drive and not stop,
to tell Jack to just keep going,
to follow the Midland Highway forever,
just the three of us.
I've had enough of this town,
and my friends
asking guilty stupid questions,
and I've had enough
of the smell of our farm
and the animals' noise,
and the winter winds whipping down Broken Lookout
and rattling our house.
I wanted to forget being pregnant
and remember being young,
like Jack and Annabel are with each other.

I was thinking all this on Saturday
in the car
when we reached Broken Lookout
where Jack parked, for the view,
and Annabel said,
"There's the farm.
It looks so beautiful at night."

Jack agreed,
and I looked at the stars,
the thousands of stars in the cold sky,
but I couldn't say a single word.

Craig hates school

I hate school.
I hate school.
I hate the kids in Year 8 and 9
who come up to me at lunch
and ask "hey, where's fat Emma.
Where's your sister, we want to try our luck."
I hate school
I can't fight the big kids,
but I do anyway.
I get one good kick, or punch,
before they clobber me,
or the teachers come.
The sooner Emma has a baby, the better.
I hate school.

A place like this

I go walking, early.
Me and my baby.
Me and my big stomach.
We walk to the channel
sit on the bank
watch the dragonflies
like mad helicopters cutting the surface.
I go walking
to avoid the kitchen
and the smell of food,
too early for cooking,
Craig and Beck arguing,
and Dad looking out the window,
thinking of money.
I go walking to watch the trees
and the sun's light filtering through them.
I talk to my baby.
I describe the farm.
I tell him about the apples
and the blossoms in spring
and the Paterson's Curse that covers the hills
and the birds gorging on rotten fruit.
I tell him everything
as we walk.
Maybe so he won't be disappointed
being born into
a place like this.

Weird

Weird

It's weird.
Very weird.
I started going to birth classes
with Emma and Jack.
I sat in the room, on the floor,
beside them.
Ten couples and the three of us.
Eleven couples holding hands, and me,
not knowing whether to touch Emma or Jack.
And Jack's weird,
he looks at me when he talks to Emma
and looks away.
He can't focus.
He's not sure who he's partner to.
He wants to help Emma I know,
so do I.
But I can't help there.
I can't be her partner,
neither can Jack,
not with me around.
So I keep away.
I stay here in the shed.
I think about Emma's baby,
and Jack.
And where Jack and I are going,

which is nowhere it seems,
and it's all too weird,
too weird to work out.

Craig and the cows

Hey, you know what?
Some Year 9 kids have painted the cows.
Farmer Austin's best dairy cows.
Each cow has a red number on its side.
Some even have sponsors!
One's sponsored by Nike!
Number 23. The Shane Warne of dairy cows!
It's all round school.
It's all round town.
There's even a photo in the newspaper,
old man Austin shaking his head,
looking at his stupid cows.
Everyone at school reckons he should
leave it on, and call them by number,
>"Number 12, your turn for milking."
>"Number 8, stop scratching against the gum tree."
Our footy coach says we should adopt one,
as a mascot.
He says we play like a bunch of cows anyway.
It's great.
The town hasn't been so happy in years.
It's great.
All over a herd of painted cows!

Annabel is ready

I'm ready.
The work is nearly done.
I want to move.
I can almost smell the road
and hear the soft hum of tyres
rolling through this year
where Jack and I plan nothing.
I'm ready. I know.

But Jack's dreaming.
He sits against the shed
reading the same page of his book
over and over.
He's looking for a reason to go,
or stay.
He walks through the house of his past,
hoping he'll find the right door,
hoping he'll find the key.

It pisses me off.
I want to go and shake him,
shake that house down.
I want to tell him he's in the wrong house,
at the wrong time.
I want to tell him we've built a new one,
with no doors locked,

no keys,
just him and me and open space.

I want to move.
Even if it's back to
sleeping in the car by the highway
with tinned food for dinner.
I don't care.
I'm ready.

*J*ack and the beach

The work is nearly done.
Once the top orchard is stripped,
we're finished.
A week, maybe two.
We've saved enough money
for six months of holiday,
camping on a beach.
I keep thinking of the one
I went to as a kid,
with Mum and Dad kissing on a towel
and my sister at the shop, talking to boys.
I want to do nothing for a long time.
No more apples,
or 7am starts.
Annabel and me.
Open fires, books to read,
bathe in the creek behind the surf,
and enough petrol in the car
to go to town whenever we want.
Annabel and me
at the beach.
And we'll get there,
we will,
after the baby.

Annabel

Jack's mad!
He thinks Emma and the baby
are his responsibility.
Uncle Jack.
Mad Uncle Jack.
He's like some crazy social worker.
Everything he touches he can fix.
I should remind him of the car!
So, what's he going to do?
Help Emma have the baby,
and then what?
Jack can't save the world,
beginning on this farm.
This is Emma's life,
she'll work it out.
Jack's got to leave it,
leave it to Emma,
and George.
They'll work it out.
Of that I'm sure.

*M*aking sense

My Mother died when I was ten.
The last time we spoke
was late in the afternoon,
after school.
She was in bed, resting,
trying to read,
and it was a beautiful day.
The sun shone right up to her bed
and she told me stories,
as well as she could —
she was heavily drugged for the pain.
And I told stories right back.
Only my stories were ones in the future.
What I planned to do.
Me and Dad and my sister.
I told her
to make her know we'd stay together,
you know, afterwards.
I didn't have a clue
what would really happen,
but I kept talking.
And one story was about grandkids.
About me and a wife and babies.
I did it for her.
I didn't want kids, I was ten years old!
I wanted my Mother, alive, and healthy.

But I made up this story,
and Mum smiled and listened,
she even laughed when I promised her
a football team of grandkids.
Then her laughing turned to coughing
and that awful sound she couldn't break.
I left her to rest.
I kissed her forehead,
the way she kissed me every night, before bed,
and I closed the door.
The sun still shone brightly ...

And that's why I go to birth classes with Emma,
why I feel I can't leave now.
Maybe it doesn't make sense.
It's like a death.
Or a birth.

Annabel and the car

Last night
I got in our car
and drove.
Just me.
No Jack. No Emma.
I drove along Turpentine Road,
up to the quarry.
I parked, turned the radio up loud,
and lay back.

I figured I had two choices.
I could keep driving and not come back.
Jack can have the money, and the beach,
and whatever else he can invent.
I'd leave the car outside his house,
and go back to my life.

My other choice was to say *no* to Jack.
To simply say *no*.
The baby will be born,
with or without him here.
And Emma will be a good mother,
and there's George, and Craig, and quiet Beck.

Lots of children don't have fathers,
or mothers.
Jack should know that,
more than all of us.

Craig

Emma says
her son's not living on a farm
all his life
and he's not picking apples
or praying for rain
or busting a gut fixing things that
can't be fixed
and he's not
wearing the same shoes winter and summer
cause that's all he's got.
And Emma says
if it's a girl
she's not marrying a farmer
or cooking all day
for kids who vomit it all back up
and she's not spending nights
watching TV and dreaming,
or getting pregnant at sixteen
and looking after brothers and sisters
and fathers and family.
Emma says all this
and I'm thinking this baby
better be born soon
because it's got a lot of living to do
and a lot of learning on what
not to do.

Birth classes

Ten farmers in flannelette shirts
and me
sit on our knees in a circle
at the CWA Hall.
Ten farmers' wives lean back
against their husbands.
Emma leans against me.
I hold her hands in mine
and talk quietly,
repeating the Instructor's words.
Sometimes I add my own.
Silly stuff like
"she'll write books
    she'll call you Mum, and me Uncle Jack
    she'll grow up smart.
    He'll grow up smart
    he'll never pick apples."
I just talk away.
Emma holds my hand tighter,
offering me encouragement.
I don't care what the farmers think.
I hold Emma's hands and talk.
We both close our eyes,
    and listen.

The perfect sky

I stop the car
a few kilometres from the farm,
at Broken Lookout.
Emma and I sit on the warm bonnet
and look at the distant farm lights.
We don't say much.
Birth classes take it all.
I tell Emma about my Mother.
Dead. Eight years now.
I tell her how I remember everything about her.
Her hair, her soft voice in the dark,
her way of looking at my sister and me.
I tell Emma I'll never forget a thing.
Not because my Mum's dead.
Not because I miss her.
But because she's my Mum
and it's important.
And before she died,
she taught me that.
She taught me what's important,
and what isn't.
And I've never forgotten.
And that's what mothers do, I say.
We look at the lights some more
under the perfect sky.
I try to remember every detail
of what's important.

Annabel and George

Jack and Emma were at birth classes last night.
I was in the shed, again.
Reading. Dreaming really,
of the beach,
of the world away from apples.
And George knocks at the door of his own shed.
He wants to talk.

He's worried Emma will leave, after the baby.
After we go.
She'll leave this farm, this land,
and him, and Craig, and Beck,
and home.
George is scared.
His voice is tight, his eyes darting.

I tell him to wait.
I tell him to look at Emma
and how she walks
and how she holds her stomach when she walks
as if she's protecting the child
as if she's afraid to let something precious fall.

I tell George to trust his daughter
and her hands.
I tell him those hands won't fail.
And I pray I'm right.

Annabel

After George left
I couldn't read anymore.
I sat on the haybales
and tried to work things out.
But all I could think was that
I felt like an intruder,
here on the farm.
For weeks we'd been helpers.
When George couldn't get pickers,
we worked.
When Emma needed someone for classes,
we volunteered.
But now,
with George wandering his farm,
like a lost man,
waiting for Emma and Jack to come home,
I knew.
We were intruding.
It was all too private.
Maybe we were wrong,
wrong to offer with the classes,
I'm not sure.
Only now, maybe,
they needed each other,
not us.

Craig and his mad dad

I think Dad's going mad!
True.
Last night I saw him
wandering around the house
in his overalls and slippers.
It was a full moon
so I could see good
and you know what they say
about a full moon — it makes you mad!
Well, Dad's walking around the yard,
and he wanders out to the orchard.
He picks an apple,
a big juicy apple,
and I think,
fine, he's going to eat it.
But no.
He starts tossing it in the air,
higher and higher
and he catches it every time.
Now Dad hardly ever throws balls
and never but never throws apples.
He's always telling me
not to drop them into the bin
in case they bruise,
and here he is, a full moon,
playing catch with an apple.

Very weird.
He's out in the orchard forever it seems,
just walking around,
with this apple,
tossing it from one hand to the other.
And this is the best bit —
he walks back to the house
and he looks up
and sees me at the window.
I'm thinking I'm going to get it
for being up so late,
but all he does is cup his hands,
like this,
meaning he wants me to catch the apple.
So I lean right out the window
and Dad throws it, perfect!
I catch it with both hands.
I take a big crunchy bite
and Dad smiles
and waves goodnight.

It was a good apple too.
A good apple, picked by a madman,
on a full moon night.

Craig and cricket

At school today,
Sports Day,
we had our cricket final
against Blairthorn School.
Most of the school were there,
you know,
cheering us on.
I got out for a duck.
I lifted my head, as usual,
and got clean bowled.
But when Blairthorn were batting,
and it was getting tight,
their best batsmen
hit this huge shot
and it was going for four, or maybe six,
and I ran around the boundary,
dived full-length, sideways,
and caught it!
Everyone cheered,
and my duck was forgotten,
and now we stood a chance of winning.

It was a good catch,
my second good catch in 24 hours,
don't you reckon?

*E*mma and the right way

I've been thinking hard.
It's all I can do right now.
Think. And wait.

I needed Jack and Annabel
on this farm two months ago.
They came out of nowhere,
and gave me hope.
The way they were, together.
Everything they do is positive.
They're not like the kids at school.
I needed them.
I needed help with birth classes.
But now,
I've been thinking about Dad.
I've never thought about him.
He just was.
I worried about Mum, wherever she is.
I worried about Beck and Craig, without Mum.

But Dad, look at him.
Three children, no wife,
a farm that barely pays
and he gets up every morning
sits on the veranda
watching the sunrise

and he counts himself lucky.
And when I come home pregnant
he doesn't yell, or rant, or blame.
He just keeps on going.
He looks almost proud of me.
Now he worries I'll leave.
He worries Jack and Annabel leaving
will mean I'll follow,
maybe not after them, but away,
anywhere.
But he's not saying anything.
He's going to let me choose,
I know.
It's his way.
It's the right way.

Guts

Maybe I don't have the guts to leave.
It shouldn't be too hard.
Mum left.
She packed and was gone in a day.
Vanished.
I could do that,
only I'd write, and phone,
and maybe come back,
you know, later.
A girl, pregnant or not,
could get lost in the city.
And it couldn't be worse than here,
could it?
Bloody Mum. I hate her.
I hate her for going so easy.
For going and staying away.
Craig and Emma still hope she'll come back,
someday.

I can see it now.
I leave home
   for the city
   I'm walking down the street
   and guess who's walking towards me
   and what do I say to her
   "hello Mum"

or
"hello Grandma."
Now that would be funny.
So funny I'd have to stop myself
from hitting her,
from telling her what I really think,
but maybe I don't have the guts
for that either.
But when I look at this farm
I keep thinking
it's not whether I have the guts to go
but
if I have the guts to stay.

*E*mma and leaving

Last night
Jack told me about the beach,
and his plans,
and the more he talked,
the more nervous I got.
I don't know why.
I can't tell.

I just listened.
I listened and dreamed.

And that's what I'm doing now.
I'm dreaming.
Only sometimes it's hard dreaming
when
Beck needs help with her homework
and Craig's talking nonstop
and Dad's burning the dinner
and my own kid's kicking his way around my belly.

So I'm not thinking good
when Beck,
bloody Beck,
she who never says a word,
looks up at me over the pages
and says

"you're smart,
you know that Emma?"

And it all makes sense,
even to smart old Emma.

A Young Orchard

A *young orchard*

It wasn't what Beck said,
but that she said it at all.
I knew.
I'm staying here.
No dreams of fancy clothes
 and cafes
 and movies
 and working in a sleek office tower.
It was old lino
and peeling paint
and apple pies every dessert
and my baby eating apple mush
and Craig and Beck and Dad.
But it was more than that,
it was me.
Me without Jack and Annabel
and some excuse to leave.
Me without Mum and the fear
of loneliness and boredom.
Me, making my way.
And Joseph, or Josephine.
Me, back at school.
Me, taking that bloody bus
 the twenty kilometres
 and the baby in childcare

while I study hard,
harder than ever before.
And me getting out of here,
my way,
when I'm ready,
with my child.
Me, getting out but
not like Mum,
running so fast
she's too scared to look back.
Me, getting out but
being able to come back.
Me and my home.
Me and the baby,
happy in the orchard
picking those stupid apples
if we choose.
Or me and my baby
leaving
finding another orchard
a young orchard
and making it ours.

Annabel

When we first came here
Jack and I had a picnic every Sunday.
We went to the channel
or across town to Brown Creek.
We lay on the blanket in the sun,
and slept. Or drank a few bottles,
and dived into the chill water.

Today we asked Emma along
and she said no.
She said no in a strange way,
and I think I know what she meant.

Here at Brown Creek
I lean over and pick up a few rocks.
I aim for a boulder on the far side of the creek.
I say to myself, as Jack sleeps,
if the first one hits
we leave this week
and drive, non-stop, to the beach.

I choose the biggest rock
and let rip,
and my aim is true.

Now

Jack wakes,
and I tell him of the boulder
and my perfect aim.

I tell him I've decided,
we leave this week.
We fill the car with petrol now,
just to be sure.

I tell him I'm not angry,
or crazy.
I tell him I'm ready,
and he should be too.
I tell him to think of our two years together.
Think of us leaving Uni and ending up here.
Think of us making love on a stack of haybales.
Think of the mornings in the orchard
and the taste of dew-fresh apples.
Think of him and me and Emma at birth classes.
Think of Craig and his painted cows.
Think of Emma here on the farm
and the rich soil of family.

And it makes sense, I know.
I hit the boulder with one throw,
and it made a strong ringing sound,
that echoed back across the creek.
We're leaving.

Emma and her Dad

Jack and Annabel
have filled their car with petrol, at last,
and gone on a Sunday drive.
A picnic, like young lovers.
They asked me along.
I said no.
I said, stay young lovers together,
and they looked at me funny.

Dad's working on the tractor, again.
Beck and Craig are in the treehouse,
playing quiet, for a change.
I take Dad some tea,
and this cake I made,
which wouldn't win any prizes
but it's OK —
I don't want to be a cook or anything.

Me and Dad sit by the tractor,
the dogs hang around for food
and the afternoon settles
on an orchard stripped of fruit.
The season is over.
Jack and Annabel can go whenever they like.
They've been waiting,
the whole farm's been waiting,
waiting for me to have this baby.

I start talking to Dad
about my baby
about Mum leaving us
and never coming back.
I tell him about school
and the long afternoons in Maths
when I dreamed myself away,
away anywhere.
And about Jack and Annabel,
smart and ready
and I'm wondering where all that smart comes from
and I figure some from parents,
some from school, and some from a place inside you.
I tell Dad
I got smart from him,
and I'm smart deep inside,
but from school I got nothing but pregnant.

I can curse school for that or curse myself,
but what's the point.
So I think school deserves more
and I say to Dad
I want to go back to school
after the baby
and for the first time in a while
Dad looks straight at me

and I'm scared to look back
because I'm not sure what it means
so I keep talking.
I tell him I rang Childcare in town
and I rang the Department
and I know it'll be hard
but it won't cost much
for the baby to be looked after
while I'm in school
and I know I can manage it
maybe even Beck and Craig can help.
I know I can do it
and I keep talking
afraid to look at Dad
and I say
Jack and Annabel should go,
go to their beach,
before the baby, who's taking his own good time.
I'll tell them thanks
and I'll promise an invitation
to the Christening.
I look straight at Dad now
knowing I have to
and he's still looking back.
I tell him when Jack goes

I'll need help with birth classes
and maybe he could come along
and he smiles.
I think it's a Dad smile.
He leans over
and takes another slice of cake
and he keeps smiling
and he says,
calm as you please
"You make a good cake Emma
  a good cake"
and I know everything will be fine,
just fine.
So I reach for a slice
to feed my baby
and myself.
I take a big slice.

A Full Tank

Craig knows

Me and Beck,
we're gunna miss you two.
We reckon you're lucky,
leaving here to spend all your time
on some beach.
Maybe we can visit
on school holidays or something?
You let us know OK?

I'm gunna miss you two.
I like the way you get drunk
every Saturday night
when you think the farm's asleep.
I like the way
you sleep late on Sunday
and stumble out of the shed
like two old drunks.
But most of all I like
the way you spend your nights
up there, on the haybales.

Yeah, that's right,
one night I couldn't sleep
and I came out here, real quiet,
so yeah,
now I know what you do in our shed!

It's time

We've packed the car,
Annabel and me.
I've filled the tank with petrol,
this time, we won't stop.

I wander into the orchard, alone.
I'm looking for the first tree I stripped,
two months back.
I'm sure I'll remember which one.
It was on the end of a line,
the highest on the farm.
The view looked over the valley and the hills,
and all the way to Broken Lookout.
I climb the tree,
and sit for a while.
The rotting fruit covers the grass
and the leaves are starting to drop.
I hear a crow up in the fir trees,
and a semitrailer on the distant highway.
And I can hear my Dad's voice
telling me to go, just go.

I hear Annabel's footsteps,
coming through the grove
and I know
that my world echoes with her sound

and that I should follow it,
the way Emma will follow her baby,
hopeful, and sure,
and tied to this farm
and these people.
I know
that today,
with a full tank,
and with Annabel,
that it's time to go.

Annabel and the orchard

Jack's up some tree.
Dreaming.
I hope the branch breaks
and he lands on his head.
That's how I feel sometimes.
But I'm glad we argued over leaving.
Sometimes you need to make a choice.
Like giving up Uni.
Like coming to this farm to work.
Like Emma getting drunk one night,
waking up pregnant,
and still saying yes to the baby
after all that.
Like me and Jack now, together,
going.
Starting now.
Starting today.
When we leave this orchard.
That is, if I can get my love, the mad bastard,
out of the tree.

Warm

*F*or the sun

It's the first rain of the season.
I think of Jack and Annabel
on some beach. I hope the sun shines there.
I can hear Dad chopping wood,
ready for a long cold spell
with frost on the orchard
cracking under our feet.
The clouds have covered the hills
and the trees are stark winter bones.
I touch my stomach, gently,
feel such power and weight
but if I get any bigger
they'll need a wheelbarrow
to get me to hospital.
I love my baby.
I don't care how it happened.
I don't care how cold this winter gets.
I stand on the veranda
and feel warmer than I've ever felt.
The wind rattles the shed door
to remind me of Jack and Annabel.
I hope they're swimming naked
in clear salty water.
I'm glad they came.
I can see Craig and Beck
walking home from the highway.

Craig's swinging his lunatic school-bag
and Beck's wandering slow, in no hurry.
I sit on the squatter's chair
put my feet up on the veranda railing,
lean back, close my eyes,
and wait, for the sun.